"Is it time for my garden party to begin?" Lady ~~Tusk~~ asked ~~her~~ butler, Tyrone. "I can't wait to show off my famous collection of priceless jewelled eggs!"

"Look, my lady," Butler Tyrone answered. "Here come your first guests."

"May I present the world-famous Detective Pablo and his assistant, Inspector Uniqua," Butler Tyrone said.

"Detective Pablo! Inspector Uniqua! I'm so glad you are here, just in case something mysterious happens!" said Lady Tasha.

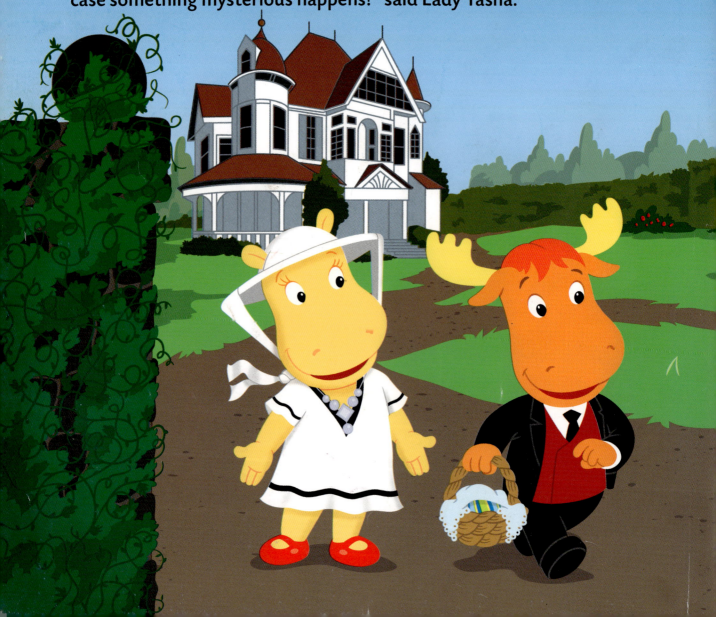

The BACKYARDIGANS™

The Mystery of the Jewelled Eggs

adapted by Lara Bergen
inspired by a teleplay by Janice Burgess
illustrated by Warner McGee

Based on the TV series *Nick Jr. The Backyardigans*™ as seen on Nick Jr.

SIMON AND SCHUSTER
First published in Great Britain in 2008 by Simon & Schuster UK Ltd
Africa House, 64-78 Kingsway, London WC2B 6AH

Originally published in the USA in 2007 by Simon Spotlight,
an imprint of Simon & Schuster Children's Division, New York.

A CIP catalogue record for this book is available from the British Library

ISBN 978-1-84738-221-4

Printed in China

10 9 8 7 6 5 4 3 2 1

Visit our websites: www.simonsays.co.uk
www.nickjr.co.uk

"Butler Tyrone, please take their things and put the eggs in the gazebo until I'm ready for them," she continued.

"At once!" replied Butler Tyrone, dashing off towards the gazebo.

"Your butler seems to be in quite a hurry, Lady Tasha," exclaimed Detective Pablo. "That's mysterious."

"Is it?" asked Lady Tasha.

"Yes. Very mysterious," replied Detective Pablo, looking back towards the gazebo.

On his way back from the gazebo, Butler Tyrone stopped at the gate to greet Lady Tasha's final guest. "May I present Mr Austin Frothingslosh," he announced.

"I'm so glad you could come," Lady Tasha greeted her neighbour. "Butler Tyrone, please take Mr Frothingslosh's hat."

"Yes, my lady," replied the butler.

"Lady Tasha," said Mr Frothingslosh, "I can't wait to see these jewelled eggs you've told me so much about."

"Well, now that everyone is here, I'll go get them!" Lady Tasha exclaimed.

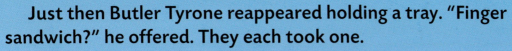

Just then Butler Tyrone reappeared holding a tray. "Finger sandwich?" he offered. They each took one.

"That butler is very mysterious! He seems to appear and disappear at the drop of a hat!" Detective Pablo remarked.

"Very mysterious," observed Mr Frothingslosh.

"I agree," Inspector Uniqua added. "But his sandwiches are delicious!"

Suddenly someone screamed. It was Lady Tasha.
"My precious eggs!" she exclaimed. "They're gone!"

"Never fear, Lady Tasha!" said Detective Pablo. "I'm on the case. Come on, Inspector Uniqua. It's time to hunt for clues. I'll bet we won't have to look far. I have already noticed some very mysterious things!"

"Well, well, well . . . what do we have here?" Detective Pablo murmured. "*This* must be our first clue."

"Great Caesar's ghost!" said Mr Frothingslosh. "That's my hat!"

"Yes, it is," Detective Pablo said. "But that's not all."

"Just as I thought!" said Detective Pablo. "Is this one of your missing eggs?"

"Yes, it is!" said Lady Tasha. "Mr Frothingslosh stole my eggs?"

"No," Detective Pablo answered, handing the egg to Lady Tasha. "Follow me."

Detective Pablo continued walking across the garden.
"Aha!" he declared, bending to pick up another jewelled egg from
behind the fountain. "Another egg . . . and another clue."

"Hey . . . what's my glove doing here?" exclaimed Inspector Uniqua.
"Mysterious, isn't it?" asked Detective Pablo, leading the way.

Soon Detective Pablo knelt down again, this time just outside Lady Tasha's gazebo. "Here is our final clue," he announced. "This handkerchief."

"Detective Pablo, isn't that *your* handkerchief?" cried Inspector Uniqua.

"Yes!" responded Detective Pablo, revealing another jewelled egg.
"And look what was hiding beside it!"
"*You* stole my eggs, Detective Pablo?" Lady Tasha exclaimed.
"Of course not!" said Detective Pablo.

"Who do you think took them?" asked Inspector Uniqua.
"Oh, I don't *think*," said Detective Pablo. "I *know* who the culprit is."
"Who?" cried the others.

"It was the butler!" said Detective Pablo.
"The butler!" Inspector Uniqua gasped. "But how do you know?"

Detective Pablo took a deep breath. "The eggs were in the basket when Lady Tasha asked the butler to bring it to the gazebo. No one went into the gazebo after him. And the eggs were already missing when he appeared with sandwiches. Plus, we all saw that he was acting very mysterious!" he explained.

"But what about my glove and your handkerchief?" Inspector Uniqua asked.

"And my hat!" Mr Frothingslosh added.

"Elementary, my dear Uniqua," Detective Pablo continued. "He was in such a hurry that he didn't put away our coats first. So he must have accidentally dropped our things when he bent down to hide the eggs."

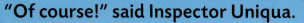

"Of course!" said Inspector Uniqua.

"One mystery remains. Why did you do it?" Detective Pablo asked the butler.

"Lady Tasha and I thought having an egg hunt would make the party more fun!" Butler Tyrone confessed.

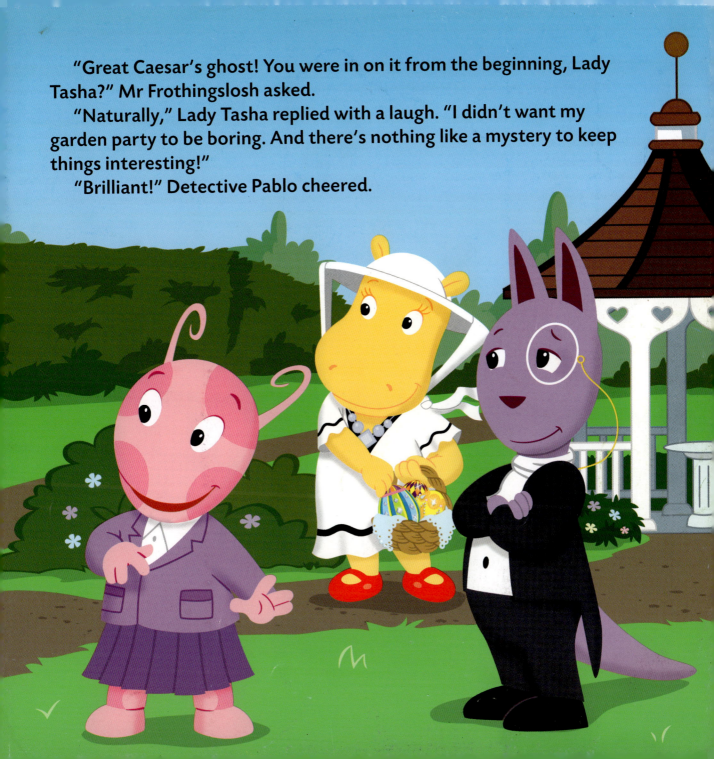

"Great Caesar's ghost! You were in on it from the beginning, Lady Tasha?" Mr Frothingslosh asked.

"Naturally," Lady Tasha replied with a laugh. "I didn't want my garden party to be boring. And there's nothing like a mystery to keep things interesting!"

"Brilliant!" Detective Pablo cheered.

Just then a mysterious rumbling sound came from Tyrone's tummy.
"Aha!" said Pablo. "I believe someone could use a snack!"
"Hiding all those eggs did make me a little hungry," admitted Tyrone.
So they all headed home for a mystery snack!